Scrapbooks of America™

Published by Tradition Books® and distributed to the school and library market by The Child's World®
P.O. Box 326, Chanhassen, MN 55317-0326 — **800/599-READ** — *http://www.childsworld.com*

Photo Credits: Cover: Bettmann/Corbis; American Philosophical Society Library: 9; Bettmann/Corbis: 6, 13, 15, 18, 24, 25, 28, 30, 34, 35; Corbis: 21, 22 (left), 38, 39, 41; Royalty-Free/Corbis: 22 (right); Joseph Sohm;Chromo Sohm Inc./ Corbis: 7, 16; Mutter Museum of the College of Physicians of Philadelphia: 10, 11; Stock Montage: 12, 17, 32

An Editorial Directions book
Editorial Directions, Inc.: E. Russell Primm, Editorial Director; Lucia Raatma, Line Editor, Photo Selector, and Additional Writing; Katie Marsico, Assistant Editor; Olivia Nellums, Editorial Assistant; Susan Hindman, Copy Editor; Susan Ashley, Proofreader; Alice Flanagan, Photo Researcher and Additional Writer

Design: The Design Lab

Library of Congress Cataloging-in-Publication Data
Cataloging-in-Publication data for this title has been applied for and is available from the United States Library of Congress.

Printed in the United States of America.

Scrapbooks of America™

The Doctor's Boy

A Story about Valley Forge in the Winter of 1777–1778

by Pamela Dell

TRADITION BOOKS®
A New Tradition in Children's Publishing™
MAPLE PLAIN, MINNESOTA

Table of Contents

There was a long, terrible groan, and a thick bubble of blood erupted from the man's mouth, followed by a gurgling sound back in his throat. Then he lay still. Another one gone. I put my fingers to his eyelids and closed them gently. There were already hundreds dead since our arrival the month before at our winter **encampment** in Valley Forge. It seemed I had begun witnessing death on a daily basis, but it had become no easier for me.

"Where's the doctor's boy?" I heard someone call from the other end of the hut.

I placed the dead soldier's arms crosswise against his bony chest. Then I looked up and said, "Here I am, sir."

I stood, rubbing a **cinder** from my eye.

These and hundreds of other soldiers were stationed at Valley Forge for the winter of 1777–78.

The British troops were in Philadelphia during the winter of 1777–1778. So Washington and his army camped at Valley Forge, about 20 miles (3.2 kilometers) away, to keep an eye on them.

The log buildings at Valley Forge were small, and the living quarters had no windows.

Our hastily built "flying hospitals" stood two each at the center of every **regiment** camped at Valley Forge, as ordered by our commander in chief, General George Washington. Small windows had been cut into the log walls, and each hut had a stone fireplace built into an end wall to lessen the cold. But the fireplaces gave off more smoke than heat or light. It was just the same in our smaller but similarly structured living quarters, though these had no windows at all. So my eyes always burned when I was inside.

Outside, though, conditions were even worse. The bitter January wind whistled and howled. Its fierce tongue reached into the huts through every opening, biting mercilessly at us all. My only comfort was that I was one of the few who had a pair of boots still wearable. They were sturdy boots made by my uncle, a **cobbler**, the year before in Massachusetts. Soon I'd outgrow them, I knew. But for the time being, I felt fortunate that I could still get my feet into them at all—and that they still had soles to keep the snow from getting in. This was not the case for nearly three thousand of the soldiers camped at Valley Forge. These poor souls not only had no shoes at all, but barely any stockings, jackets, or **breeches** to cover them either. We were mostly all in rags and sorely unfit to meet the unbearable cold. But my duties in the hospital did not leave much time to grumble about it.

~

Upon seeing me rise, the captain who had spoken motioned me to him, and I went quickly. As I passed the rows of bunks, a few of the sufferers called out to me in weak voices. They **bid** me come to their side in aid, but for the moment, I had to close my ears to them and obey the captain, as he had been appointed by the commanding officer to check daily on our hospital. He was standing at the bedside of a man whose body looked like nothing more than a skeleton covered by a stretch of thin, gray skin and a few strips of clothing. Terrible **pustules** dotted the man's bare arms and his face. But I had seen worse. Much worse.

"What's your name, boy?" the officer asked.

Flying hospitals were usually 15 feet (4.5 meters) wide and 25 feet (7.6 m) long and only 9 feet (2.7 m) high. There were windows on each side and a chimney on one end.

Head Quarters V: F:

Major Genl. tomorrow DeKalb. Brigadier Varnum

Field Officers Lt. Coll. Burr, Major Nichols Brigade Majr. McClinton

The Honourable the Congress having been pleased to call Coll. Pickering to a seat at the Board of war, have appointed Coll. Scammell Adjudant Genl. in his room, who is to be obeyed and respected as such. Officers Commanding Guards are to give the Countersigns to the Picquets as soon as it is dark.— The Commander in Chief is surprised to hear that the Butchers have extorted money from the Soldiers for the plucks of Beef The Commissaries are therefore directed to Issue the plucks and heads together for 8 pounds, and the Quarter Masters are to see that the different Companies draw it by turn, The Flying Hospital Hutts are to be 15 feet wide and 25 long in the clear and the story at least 9 feet high to be covered with boards or shingles only without any dirt, Windows made on each side and a Chimney at one end, Two such Hospitals are to be made for each Brigade at or near the Center and if the ground permits of it not more than 100 yards distance from the Brigade.

Head Quarters V: F: January 14th 1778.

On January 13, 1778, one of the officers at Valley Forge recorded this entry in his daily journal. He described the flying hospitals built at the encampment.

"Eleazor Portis, sir. What need have you?"

"Where is the regiment doctor who oversees this hut?"

"'Tis Monday, sir. He is making his weekly report on the condition of our patients, as General Washington has instructed. He is soon to return, I'm certain."

"Let us hope so," the officer replied. "But in the meantime, these men back here, what is being done for them?"

"This one's wounds are not healing well, sir," I said in a low voice. "And he has the Itch as well. He should be prescribed **sulfur** baths but we have no supplies at all. Nor any hog's **lard** even to make an **ointment**."

The Itch is a disease also known as impetigo, a contagious skin condition.

Dr. William Shippen Jr. served as the director general of all military hospitals for the Continental army. He and the other doctors worked hard to help sick and wounded soldiers.

Putrid Fever is an illness also known as typhus, a bacterial disease causing delirium, headaches, and rashes.

Doctors used all sorts of tonics and medical instruments to treat the troops.

The officer looked at me curiously, as if inspecting my every feature. I turned away and bent over the sick man, carefully drawing the threadbare blanket up to his chin.

"How long have you apprenticed?" the officer now asked.

"Two years," I replied, my back still to him. In reality it had only been one year that I had officially worked as a surgeon's mate. But I had first spent another year training with my own father, a forward-thinking man, before he had been taken himself, by the evil known as **Putrid Fever.**

"And you are how old?" the officer persisted.

Before I could make my answer, one of the regiment doctors, Doctor Fish, strode in through the doorway and approached us. Close on his heels was William Wormish, another surgeon's mate from Massachusetts like myself. Seeing me standing with the officer, Wormish brushed his hand sharply under his nose and then shook it, as if tossing away something disagreeable from his fingers. I knew the insult meant by his crude gesture, but I chose, as always, to ignore him. Instead, I looked to Doctor Fish and said hello.

The doctor nodded. "The lad is but fifteen!" he said proudly to the officer, having heard his last question to me. "Small for his age, 'tis true, and uncommonly young to be carrying on this work. But he came to me already having a remarkable ability to **diagnose** and treat, and he learns rapidly, too."

When troops were recruited, they often had no idea how trying their time in the army would be.

The British troops were known as Redcoats because of the bright red uniforms they wore.

Members of the Continental army fought difficult battles against the British Redcoats.

"But are you certain he is—" The officer tried to interrupt Dr. Fish's recommendation of me but did not get far.

"We cannot afford simply to turn away such fellows when our needs here are so great, do you not agree, sir? Even one so young."

After a moment's seemingly doubtful pause, the officer nodded slightly. But his eyes stayed closely upon me, and a small frown marked his brow.

"Portis here has already proved himself many times over," the doctor reassured him. "Worth more than his weight in milk and fresh meat."

"If only we had some of those and less of him," Bill Wormish piped up sourly. He shot me an angry look. But Dr. Fish and the captain were already engaged in conversation about the poor conditions in which we worked, so Bill Wormish's remark escaped them. It was my opportunity to slip past them all and go to the bedside of a patient who was calling out for me.

I took a stool beside him, a man called Joshua Tennant. He had lain for two weeks in a deep fever. When it was available, I had made him a mixture of thin **barley** water to drink. I had even **bled** him more than once myself, in an attempt to drain the fever from his bloodstream. Finally, just that morning, his temperature had begun to cool and he was at last coming out of his **delirium.**

But there remained a physical terror for him much worse than fever. As one of the many troops who had no shoes, he had walked barefoot from Whitemarsh to Gulph Mills, and then on to Valley Forge in the middle of December. As our scraggly Patriot army made its way against the sleet and the blowing snow, over ice-covered roads and frozen **gullies,** we left a bloody trail of footprints that marked the way we had come. The weather had been so bad and the conditions so severe that it had taken us an entire week to walk only thirteen miles.

We had arrived at our winter campgrounds in Valley Forge, chosen by General Washington, on December 19, 1777. There had been no shelter of any kind to protect us, only the trees above and a few tents. So the men had huddled about fires each night,

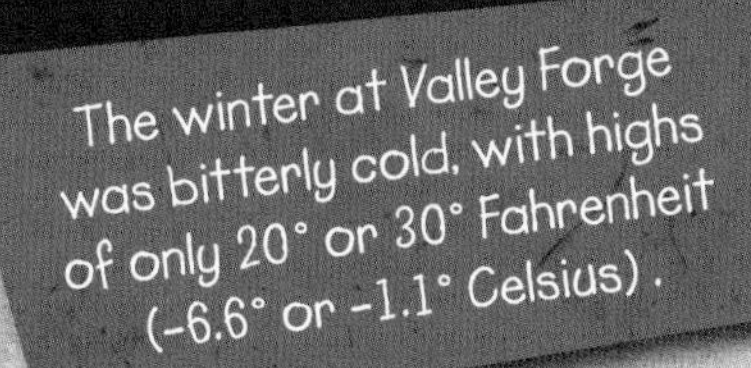

The winter at Valley Forge was bitterly cold, with highs of only 20° or 30° Fahrenheit (-6.6° or -1.1° Celsius).

George Washington served as commander in chief of the Continental army. He and his troops faced a long, cold winter at Valley Forge.

trying to stay warm, trying to stay alive, until living quarters could be built. Within a month, most of the men were sleeping in huts, during which time they gained the greatest respect for General Washington. The general left his own canvas tent and took up residence in a village home only after every soldier was already housed. His extreme concern over the conditions in camp kept him writing urgent letters to Congress almost daily, Dr. Fish had told me, requesting aid of all kinds. But the men continued to freeze, starve, suffer, and die.

Joshua Tennant was not the only soldier over the past month whose feet had turned to ice. But, like many others, his had not thawed. Rather, they had turned black. And then

Before the log buildings were made, troops were housed in simple canvas tents.

Soldiers faced various injuries in battle. Some even lost legs or arms.

The troops arrived at Valley Forge in time for Christmas in 1777. But there was no food for a proper holiday dinner. Instead the men had only cold water and fire cakes (a batter of flour and water fried on a griddle).

green, which indicated the deathly infection. Finally, Dr. Fish had had to **amputate** both of Joshua's feet just above the ankles, to keep the infection from spreading to his entire body. I had had to muster all my courage to act as the doctor's assistant in these surgeries. We had no remedies to ease the pain, so I, Bill Wormish, and others had used all our strength to hold Joshua down while he bit a **musket ball** to keep from screaming in agony or swallowing his tongue.

Now, nearly every night in my dreams, I heard the ghastly screams of suffering men. I saw men losing limbs, men blind and choking from disease. Once-able soldiers stretched frail from starvation on cots and rough bunks. But each morning I would go

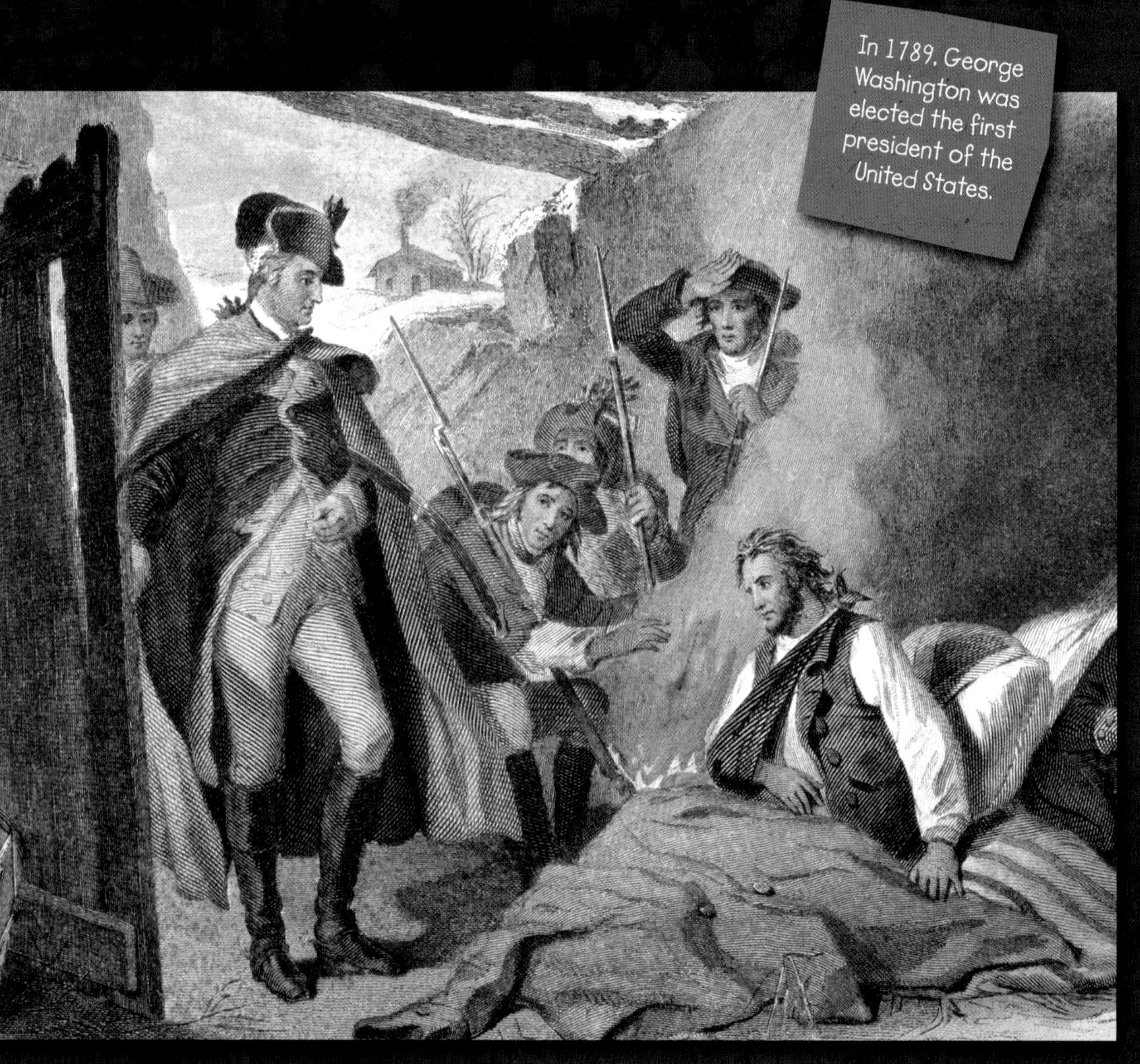

In 1789, George Washington was elected the first president of the United States.

The troops at *Valley Forge* appreciated the time General Washington took to visit and speak with them.

on with my medical duties. I would never go back to the life I had left.

The grace and goodness of General Washington had kept some remarkable shred of spirit alive in his troops, and my own spirit was truly fiercely alive. Despite the lack of food, clothing, and medical supplies, and having not even the warmth of decent living quarters, these men hung on. If they could do it, I would, too. Despite the horrors, they seemed, man after man, determined to survive so that they might fight the Redcoats to the very end. It was, to me, something of a miracle, and the greatest part of that miracle was that so many would endure such trials in the faint hope of defeating the mighty British military. But it was that dream of freeing ourselves and living in peace as an independent nation that drove us on. So far there had been very few deserters, and Washington had even managed to ease every hint of **mutiny.**

Lying weak on the hard wooden slats of his bed, and with only a thin layer of straw to cover him, Joshua watched me with haunted eyes. He held out his hand. I grasped it and squeezed, then put a sponge to his forehead.

"You have peace in your eyes," he said. His voice was only a hoarse, weak whisper. "If you were my child, I should not allow you to witness such sights as are to be seen in this place . . ." His voice trailed away and then came back. "I had a child once—she had the same peace in her eyes as you do,

Portis. I feel her close when I look at you."

"Hush now," I said. "Don't tire yourself, Mr. Tennant." I looked around to note what the captain and the doctor were up to, and I saw they had moved together to the bed of the dead man. Doctor Fish was removing what clothing the man had on, to be kept for some other soldier in need. The body would be buried naked, I knew, as they always were, for this reason.

But Bill Wormish was watching me. I turned back to my patient as he spoke again.

"Why has your father let you be here, Portis?" Joshua persisted. "You are too young yet. 'Tis not right. If you must be here, 'twould be better that you were a **fife** player, or a drummer boy."

"Hush," I repeated. "You must stay quiet now, sir."

I did not want to argue with an ailing man, but inside my temper flared. I was here with good reason. I could tend the ill, and do so with more ability than nearly anyone my age. I had learned my skills at Pa's side, and my being here honored both him and the Patriot cause, too. And where else should I be now? Back in Massachusetts tending only the fire with my mother? Caring instead for my three small, squalling siblings? Taking orders from a stepfather who believed I should be waiting on him day and night and following tradition rather than following my own heart? No, I would have none of it!

Dr. Fish had gone out with the captain

Young men playing fifes and drums sometimes led American troops into battle.

A number of young boys played drums and fifes in the army. These accompanied some of Washington's soldiers.

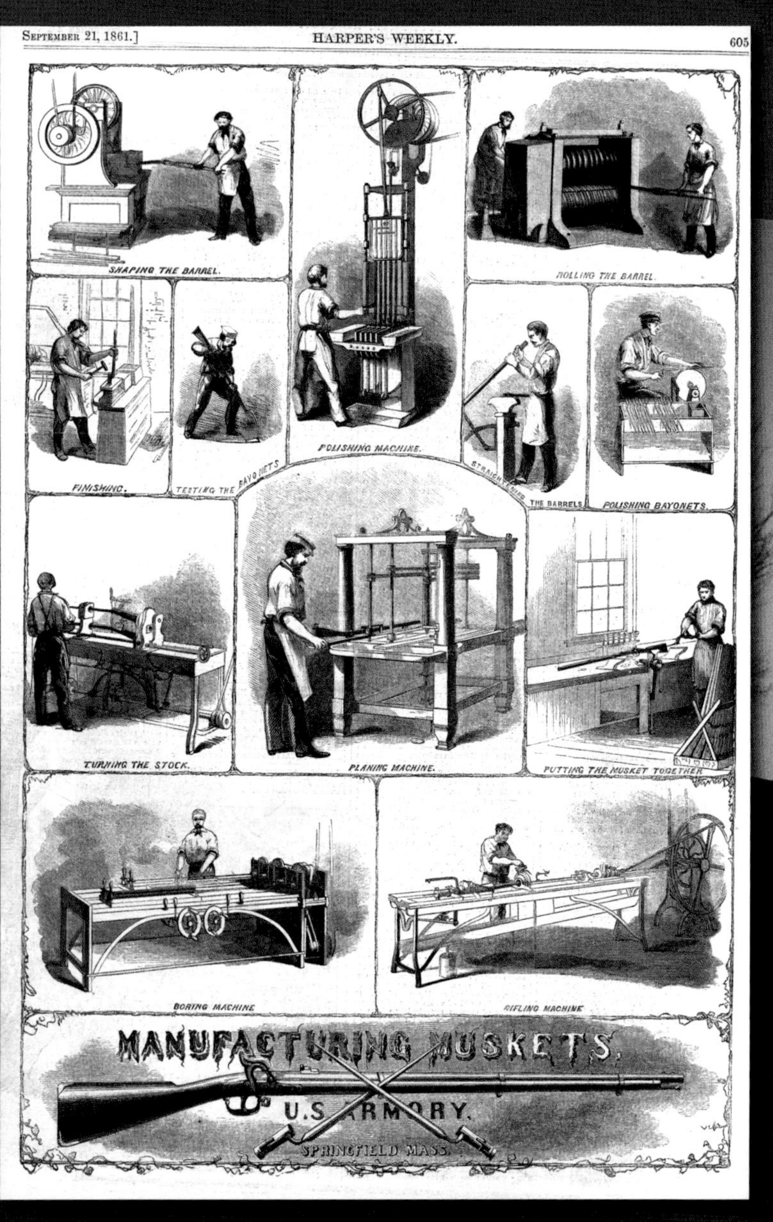

Muskets were important weapons for soldiers in the American Revolution.

A musket was a type of gun used by the army during the American Revolution. Many were 6 or 7 feet long (1.8 or 2.1 m) and weighed 40 pounds (18 kilograms).

Troops also fought with cannons.

and now returned alone. He went to the bedside of one of the sickest in the hut and peered down at him in the dim light. The man had a **splint** on his thigh that I knew Bill Wormish had helped apply. Dr. Fish released the straps holding the splint in place and examined his patient.

"We shall need to re-break this bone, as it is not setting properly," I heard him say. "Portis, come. Give me a hand here!"

"I'll do it, sir," Bill said at once. "Portis is occupied." I hesitated.

"No such thing, Wormish," the doctor replied. "I need my best boy for this job. It's already been **botched** once. Portis!"

As I moved to assist Dr. Fish, I tried to avoid Bill Wormish, but he made a point of passing me by and knocking against me as he went. When the painful job was through, I hurried outside for a moment's relief. The air was sharp with cold but not fresh. A **stench** rose from many parts of our campground always, and I had to cover my face with my tattered jacket sleeve as I slipped off toward the woods. The ground was mostly frozen solid, so the smells of human waste, vomit, and the rotting flesh of unburied horses that had starved to death mixed together and hung in the air.

I had just ducked behind a tall black ash tree, out of sight of the hospital, to do some business of my own, when a hard hand grabbed my shoulder and whirled me around. It was Bill Wormish. He towered over me with all the **menace** of a black bear.

"I know you're hiding something, Portis," he snarled, "Admit it!"

Trying to show no alarm, I declared, "I've nothing to hide, Bill. Leave me be."

"Leave you be, but of course! So you can go on fooling Dr. Fish and everyone else, I suppose?! You with your high and mighty notion of being some kind of brilliant doctor—rather than what you really are!"

I stepped back, wary, and Bill came on right after me, his face squeezed together in a hateful way. He shoved my shoulder with the ball of his hand, and I stumbled back a few more steps.

There were approximately 10,000 men at the Valley Forge encampment in the winter of 1777–1778.

Most women were able to help the troops only by making clothing and sending supplies to them.

A Continental soldier in full uniform and armed with a musket

"If you don't want me telling everyone what you're hiding, Eleazor—" My name came out of Bill Wormish's mouth in a harsh, taunting way, "then you'll have to fight me for your honor!"

"I'm not fighting!" I said, turning my back to him and hoping he'd ease up enough to let me go my way.

"You are!" he shrieked. I felt his hand cold again around my upper arm. With one hard movement he flung me onto my back in the snow. The next thing I knew a scream was flying from my mouth, and I was instantly ashamed of myself. A bird rose startled from a bare branch and flew off. Bill howled with laughter.

"Silly little weakling!" he coughed,

through his fit of laughter. "You are nothing but a—"

"Bill Wormish!" another voice, up nearer the hospital, roared. Dr. Fish and two tattered soldiers were hurrying our way. I got up quickly and brushed myself off. My coat had come open as I fell, but I drew it as close around me as I could. I was shivering.

"For shame!" Dr. Fish scolded as he faced Bill. The two soldiers stood silent but watching, ready to move against Bill if given the word. "I best not see you worrying Portis one more time over anything, Wormish. If I do, you'll not only be off the medical staff for good, but you will be **court-martialed** and sent home with no muss and no fuss. And no pay. Do you hear me?"

By the spring of 1778, about one-quarter of the troops had died from starvation, poor nutrition, or disease.

I doubted Bill would ever be put on trial for simply bothering me, but I felt good that Dr. Fish seemed so sure. Bill shrugged as if he wasn't one bit afraid, but his upper teeth were cutting hard into his lower lip.

"Now you go on and get, boy!" Dr. Fish said. "Back to your job."

Immediately Bill began heading toward the huts, then he swung around and, walking backward, pointed a long finger at me.

"I know about you," he said. "So you better watch it, Portis."

And then he was gone.

~

Bill Wormish did stay clear of me for the next several weeks. Aside from the black thunderclouds that seemed to build in his eyes whenever he looked my way, he appeared to have little interest in me. But occasionally I would look up from one sickbed or another to find his eyes on me. In those times, when he knew I'd caught him watching, a small, strange smile would cross his mouth, and just as he had that day in the woods, he would point a finger at me. The only difference in his gesture now was that he did it in a much less obvious way so that, I was sure, Dr. Fish would not catch him. I tried to keep my head clear as I went about my work, but he troubled me with his cold stare and his dark, secretive interest in my business.

~

Martha Washington arrived at Valley Forge on her husband's forty-fifth birthday.

At the beginning of the second week in February, a buzz spread through our encampment. General Washington's wife, Martha, had arrived in Valley Forge. Soon we began to hear of her many kindnesses and of the woolen socks she and other ladies were knitting for the soldiers. But I did not lay eyes on her myself until she had been already ten days in the village. On that day, she appeared in the doorway of the hospital hut I was working in.

"Madam," I said, surprised, "for whom are you looking?" I was near the door at the time and noticed her before the others did. But I had not yet recognized her as Mrs. Washington. Many women camped themselves at the fringes of our 4,000 acres.

George and Martha Washington visiting the troops at Valley Forge

Some were relatives of the men and boys in camp, others just hoping to help the Patriot cause by cooking or mending or whatever they could find to do. But this woman was elegant in her manners and finely dressed. And unlike the ones in camp, she was spotlessly clean and neat looking. In a moment, I had guessed who she was. She introduced herself, confirming my suspicions, and I bowed.

"Would you be so kind as to take me around the hospitals of the regiment here, young man?" she said. "I would like to comfort the men with prayers."

I had heard of her doing this, but altogether more than 900 huts were spread over the camp grounds of Valley Forge. As far as I knew, she had never visited our two hospitals. I looked back through the smoky haze to the other end of the hospital, where Dr. Fish, Bill, and a second doctor were busy. Hearing Mrs. Washington's voice, though, the doctors looked up and came at once. As always, Bill, instead of staying at his post, was hustling along behind them.

After the greetings, it was agreed that I should be the one to accompany her through both huts, which I could see did not please Bill at all. I chose to take her around next door first, so that I would not have to endure his barely hidden rage—or possibly his rude gestures sneakily made in front of a lady. Much to my relief, by the time we returned, Bill seemed to have calmed himself. He ignored us both completely as I took Mrs. Washington around.

After quite a while of her gentle attentions to the men, during which she impressed me by showing neither fear nor disgust, I escorted her to her carriage. As we stood there in the blustery cold, with **sentries** hatless and barefooted guarding her, she held out her hand to me and I took it.

"You are a remarkable boy. It is plain that the men respect you and look forward to your presence," she said. I made a quick bow of my head to acknowledge the compliment. "There is certainly something about you, Mr. Portis. I don't quite know how to express it . . ."

"I must go back, ma'am. My duties—"

"Something familiar, somehow," Mrs.

Mrs. Washington was a kind and thoughtful woman. I enjoyed getting to meet her and show her our hospital.

Washington went on, as if I hadn't spoken. "But yet something . . . I would say . . . mysterious . . . very private, at least."

"We are so close in these quarters," I managed, "that one must keep a little bit to himself, just to survive. That is all."

Mrs. Washington smiled. "Of course. You are right, and it is wise. That's all it is, isn't it?"

" 'Tis all it is," I agreed. Then she squeezed my hand in a kind and motherly way, bid me well, and was off in her carriage. I watched her go, with many strange mixed feelings swirling in my chest.

~

During my afternoon with her, Martha Washington had told me about a Prussian officer who was coming from Europe to train our troops, a Baron von Steuben. He had apparently been hired on the recommendation of Benjamin Franklin, and each day I eagerly listened for news of his arrival. And then, at the end of February, there seemed to be a sudden new flow of energy throughout the encampment: Baron von Steuben had finally come!

Wagons were unable to bring supplies to us, for the roads were so bad. We had heard of entire barrels of clothing being left in ditches because the drivers could not pass over the frozen, muddy ruts. Nearby farmers and villagers mostly preferred to sell their food and other goods to the British for gold rather than to General Washington for the nearly worthless paper money of the Continental Congress. But with the arrival of von Steuben,

Baron von Steuben arrived at Valley Forge to help train the American soldiers.

these things began to matter less to the men in our encampment, for they had become focused on something else: Here was someone to make them into real soldiers! Once I heard his training was in progress, and changing the attitudes of one and all, my mind became fixed on seeing the baron at work myself. Finally I got my opportunity.

It was a day in early March, with a welcome hint of warmth in the air after the long brutal months of winter. Better weather, more food supplies, and the discipline of practicing von Steuben's precision drills had lifted spirits. It was as if we were in a different camp. Yet not much had changed in the hospitals.

Many with severe cases of disease had been sent to the General Hospitals in Yellow Springs and elsewhere, but some were now calling those facilities death wards. We had heard that in those places, with the ill crammed in together by the dozens, death frequently took everyone. Doctors, nurses, and patients alike. It was nearly as bad at Valley Forge, where medical supplies continued to be few, and thousands had already perished from disease.

But as I climbed the slight rise overlooking the drill field that March afternoon, I put these depressing thoughts away. Here was something to see! I found a large rock to perch on and began to watch in awe as a company of a hundred men performed their moves like one smooth, well-oiled machine. Before each step of the musket drill, von

Steuben shouted the command in French and then another soldier would repeat it in English. Some of the commands I could hear even from the distance: *Prime! Poise firelock! Take aim! Fire!*

The boom of musket fire thrilled me, for now I realized I was looking at soldiers who had become disciplined. And that discipline had given them pride and self-respect. Watching them now, changed altogether into something else, I could imagine a day in the summer soon to come. A day when our troops would head out once again to meet the Redcoats in battle. On that day these soldiers would march not as a loose band of raggedy Patriots and assorted **militia** men, but as highly trained members of the Continental

After working with von Steuben, our soldiers were more disciplined and ready for battle.

The spirit of our soldiers was important for winning independence from Great Britain.

Army. Proud and powerful rather than weak and starving. And as such they would be the downfall of the British, I was sure of it.

The thought was such an exciting one, and the sounds of the drills thrilled me so, that I leaped to my feet, raised up my arms shouting, and whirled around in a joyful dance. And then stopped dead. Bill Wormish was standing there staring at me, his arms hanging and his fists in knots.

"Bill!"

"What are you doing up here?" he said. His voice held the hiss of a snake.

When I didn't reply, he said, "You don't belong up here. You don't belong anywhere around here. *Eleazor.*"

I glanced around, but there was no one

nearby, only the men on the field yards away.

"I can be here if I like," I told him, keeping my voice even. "I'm on meal break."

"You should not even be in this camp," Bill went on. "You have no business being anywhere near the men."

"It's not up to you whether I be a surgeon's mate or not," I reminded him, but I was feeling tense. His whole body **reeked** of threat.

Bill took a step toward me and then, with a swift move I wasn't ready for, reached out, and grabbed my hair in his fist. His fingers on the back of my neck were rough and cold as he yanked with all his might. I jerked my head violently and slammed both my hands against his arm, trying to get out of his clutches. I had been given a thick dab of grease that very morning and had oiled my hair well. My braid slid easily out of his grasp. Only the ribbon I used to keep it tied was left dangling in his fingers.

Enraged that I had gotten away, Bill lunged at me again. He grabbed at my coat and attempted to rip it off. I kicked out at his shins, landed one severe blow, and then bent away from him and ran.

"You're done with!" I heard him scream behind me. But he was standing in his place, not chasing after me as I had expected. "You're no doctor! You're not even a surgeon's mate. And everyone shall know it!"

"I am a surgeon's mate!" I cried back at him, feeling braver now that I was well away from him. "A far better one than you, too!"

"You're nothing! *Nothing!*" This time

Bill's screaming words sounded even more vicious and desperate to my ears than before. "You're nothing, Portis, because I know what you really are—you're a girl!"

I stopped. Even in my fear, his words were like lead balls chained to my feet, stopping them in their tracks. A thin film had broken out across my brow, and I wiped it away with the back of my hand. Looking back at Bill Wormish, I felt sick. He stood motionless, staring down at me with hands on hips and a wide grin of evil triumph on his face.

I turned and fled.

~

After Bill Wormish found me out and reported me to Dr. Fish, the doctor confirmed the fact for himself and I was done with the Massachusetts regiments for good. Although he was greatly sorry to lose my skills, Dr. Fish said, it was highly improper for a girl to serve as anything more than a nurse, at best. He was shocked to think that I had been in such close quarters with grown men, not to mention a witness to their ailments and bodily secrets. If I would go quietly and never return, he told me, he would keep Bill Wormish in line and not have me reported. This would save me the disgrace of being drummed out of the army with all watching me go. I agreed to his terms and set off that very day.

But there were several thousand soldiers camped at Valley Forge. Brigades from each of the colonies and others besides. Who would know if Eleanor Portis turned up as Eleazor

Portis—or perhaps Eleazor Porter, just for extra safety's sake—at the far opposite end of camp and asked for work in a hospital hut there? I was a doctor in every fiber of my body and mind, something carried through from my pa to me. If I had to keep some secrets to fulfill that role, well, I would gladly do so again. And I did.

On May 5, 1778, a huge ceremony took place in camp to celebrate France's officially joining with America to battle the British. General Washington led prayers and joyfully addressed the crowd. The perfection and power of the soldiers' drills awed everyone, and all exclaimed at how they had triumphed over the worst of all hardships to become a fearsome army.

The Marquis de Lafayette, a French soldier, also met with George Washington at Valley Forge. He was eager to help the American army, so he joined the cause and fought the Redcoats without pay.

Marquis de Lafayette was one of the French soldiers who helped us fight the Redcoats.

In the 1700s, girls wore long skirts, aprons, and capes. To look like a boy, a girl would have to wear trousers and keep her hair tied up.

Article 10.

The solemn Ratifications of the present Treaty expedited in good and due Form shall be exchanged between the contracting Parties in the Space of six Months or sooner, if possible, to be computed from the Day of the Signature of the present Trea In Witness whereof We the undersigned their Ministers Plenipotentiary have in their Name and in Virtue of our full Powers, signed with our Hands the present Definitive Treaty, and caused the Seals of our Arms to be affixed thereto.

Done at Paris, this third Day of Septemb In the Year of our Lord, one thousand, seven hundre and Eighty three. –

D Hartley

John Adams

B Franklin

John Jay

When the Treaty of Paris was signed in 1783, the long war was finally over.

In 1781, British troops surrendered at Yorktown. The Americans and British signed a preliminary peace treaty the next year.

Standing there witnessing the event with the medical men of Brigadier General McIntosh's North Carolina regiment, I felt joy lifting high my own heart, too. I had made my way into their camp in mid-March and they had accepted me with wholehearted enthusiasm after I had shown a little of what I knew about their profession. I was one of them now. Watching the gun salutes, the cannons booming, and the muskets firing, I felt proud to be part of this historic day, and I was well satisfied with my progress in doctoring. Even better than these feelings, though, I held a sly and private satisfaction that my secret had not come wholly undone. It would remain with me for at least a while longer, and hopefully for many, many years to come.

The History of Valley Forge in the Winter of 1777–1778

During the American Revolution, fifteen-year-old Eleanor Portis became a surgeon's mate in the Continental army. In 1777, it was considered improper for young women to live in camps with men, so Eleanor disguised herself as a boy and joined the medical staff as Eleazor Portis. During the war, many such women placed themselves in harm's way to care for soldiers and serve their country.

On December 19, 1777, the Continental army arrived at their winter quarters in Valley Forge, about 30 miles (48 km) from Philadelphia, Pennsylvania. The ragtag army, under the command of General George Washington, had fought bravely against British forces at Trenton, Brandywine, and Germantown. Now the poorly dressed troops were tired, starving, and sick. Few soldiers had shoes. Their worn-out uniforms and thin blankets provided little protection from the cold.

After building huts, the soldiers settled in to rest. But the 16-by-14 foot (5-by-4 m) huts, which housed twelve men each, were drafty, damp, smoky, and unhealthy. The dirty conditions became breeding grounds for disease. Doctors faced a difficult task. The washed-out bridges and harsh winter conditions made it hard for them to get food, clothing, and medical supplies to the sick and dying. Every day, the doctors risked their lives, but they were paid very little. A surgeon received between $2 and $4 per day and four to six rations (food portions). Surgeon's mates received $1 a day and two rations.

Because sickness was so widespread in the early days of the camp, General Washington issued orders for "flying hospitals" to be constructed—two for each brigade. But the small, temporary hospitals were understaffed and lacked medical supplies. By the time the army left Valley Forge in June 1778, an estimated 3,000 men had died in camp or nearby hospitals. If it had not been for the physicians, surgeons, and surgeons' mates serving during this critical time in U.S. history, more soldiers would have died. And that tragedy might have changed the outcome of the war.

Glossary

amputate to cut off part of the body—an arm, leg, finger, etc.—usually because it is diseased

barley a type of grain

bid to ask someone to do something

bled removed blood from a person, in an attempt to rid the body of disease

botched messed up or ruined

breeches pants that cover the hips and thighs, usually fitting tightly just under the knees

cinder a small piece of ash from a fire

cobbler a person who makes or repairs shoes and other leather goods

court-martialed tried in a military court

delirium a mental state that is marked by confusion

diagnose to recognize the signs and symptoms of an illness

encampment a place where military troops camp

fife a small flute

gullies trenches worn into the ground by running water, usually from a stream

lard a soft white fat made from the tissue of a pig

Timeline

1773 On December 16, American colonists protest against British taxes by dumping tea into the Boston Harbor, an event called the Boston Tea Party.

1774 The First Continental Congress meets in Philadelphia.

1775 On April 18, Paul Revere makes his famous ride in Massachusetts to warn of the British army's advances; on April 19, fighting between the American forces and the Redcoats begins with the battles at Lexington and Concord; on May 10, the Second Continental Congress meets in Philadelphia; on June 15, George Washington is named commander in chief of the Continental army.

menace a show of danger or possible threat

militia a group of people called into military service

musket ball a metal ball used as ammunition for a musket

mutiny the act of a group of people taking control over their leader

ointment a thick, sometimes greasy substance put on the body to heal or protect it

pustules types of raised, infected blisters on the skin

Putrid Fever typhus; typhoid, a different disease, was known as Camp Fever or Malignant Bilious Fever

reeked smelled strongly

regiment a military unit often made from a number of troops

sentries soldiers that stand guard, often at entrances to buildings

splint a thin strip of wood used to keep a bone in place while it heals

stench an overwhelming odor

sulfur chemical used in treating certain skin diseases

1776 In July, the Declaration of Independence is adopted, declaring American independence from Great Britain; in December, Washington and his men cross the Delaware River and capture Trenton, New Jersey.

1777 In early December, Washington's army fights the British at Whitemarsh, Pennsylvania; in late December, Washington and his army camp at Valley Forge for the winter.

1778 On May 1st, Washington learns that France has joined an alliance with the colonies to fight the British; in June, Washington and his army leave Valley Forge.

1781 American troops win a key victory in Yorktown, Virginia.

1783 In September, the United States and Great Britain sign a peace treaty; in December, Washington resigns as commander in chief.

1787 The U.S. Constitution is adopted.

Activities

Continuing the Story

(Writing Creatively)

Continue Eleanor's story. Elaborate on an event from her scrapbook or add your own entries to the beginning or end of her journal. You might write about her relationship with her father and the medical training she received from him. Or you might focus on what her life was like after she left Valley Forge. You can also write your own short story of historical fiction about Valley Forge and the role the camp played in helping to win the Revolutionary War.

Celebrating Your Heritage

(Discovering Family History)

Research your own family history. Record the names of relatives who lived in Pennsylvania or the surrounding colonies during the American Revolution. Were they involved directly or indirectly with activities at Valley Forge? Ask family members to write down what they know about the people and events of this time period. Make copies of old drawings, or drawings of letters and keepsakes, from this era.

Documenting History

(Exploring Community History)

Find out how your city or town was affected by the American Revolution and by Valley Forge in particular. Visit your library, a historical society, a museum, or related Web sites for links to important people and events. What did newspapers report at the time? When, where, why, and how did your community respond? Who was involved? What was the result?

Preserving Memories

(Crafting)

Make a scrapbook about family life in the American colonies during the late 1770s. Or create a scrapbook about a surgeon's or a soldier's life at the time of the American Revolution. Imagine what life was like for a soldier or surgeon. Fill the pages with special events, stories, interviews with relatives, letters, and drawings of memorabilia. Include copies of newspaper clippings, postcards, posters, medical or military ledgers, diaries, and historical records. Decorate the pages and cover with keepsakes, army and medical equipment, maps, medical drawings, and pictures of famous colonial landmarks.

To Find Out More

At the Library

Stein, R. Conrad. *Valley Forge.* Danbury, Conn.: Children's Press, 1999.

Stewart, Gail B. *Life of a Soldier in Washington's Army.* Minneapolis: Lucent, 2002.

Wagoner, Jean Brown. *Martha Washington: America's First Lady.* New York: Aladdin, 1986.

On the Internet

Historic Valley Forge
http://www.ushistory.org/valleyforge
To learn more about Valley Forge
and the people who served there

The Military Journal of George Ewing: A Soldier of Valley Forge
http://www.sandcastles.net/military1.htm
To read the words of a Valley Forge soldier

On the Road

Valley Forge National Historical Park
Route 23 and N. Gulph Road
Valley Forge, PA 19482
610/783-1077
To tour the site of this famous encampment

Washington Crossing Historic Park
1112 River Road
Washington Crossing, PA 18977
215/493-4076
To see where Washington and his men crossed the Delaware River

Through the Mail

Valley Forge Convention and Visitors Bureau
600 W. Germantown Pike
Plymouth Meeting, PA 19462
610/834-1550
For information about the area and planning a trip

About the Author

Pamela Dell has been making her living as a writer for about fifteen years. Though she has published both fiction and nonfiction for adults, in the last decade she has written mostly for kids. Her nonfiction work includes biographies, science, history, and nature topics. She has also published contemporary and historical fiction, as well as award-winning interactive multimedia. The twelve books in the Scrapbooks of America series have been some of her favorite writing projects.